HELP EACH OTHER

FOREST FRIENDS HELP EACH OTHER
Text copyright © 1993 by Danae Dobson.
Illustrations copyright © 1993 by Cuitlahuac Morales.

Managing Editor: Laura Minchew
Project Editor: Beverly Phillips

Library of Congress Cataloging-in-Publication Data

Dobson, Danae.
  Forest friends help each other / Danae Dobson ; illustrated by
Cuitlahuac Morales.
     p.   cm. — Forest friends series
  "Word kids!"
  Summary: In a dream, six-year-old Eric helps his forest animal
friends rescue Pinky the rabbit when she falls into the river, after
which they discuss God's love.
  ISBN 0–8499–0986–4
  [1. Forest animals—Fiction. 2. Dreams—Fiction. 3. Christian
life—Fiction.] I. Morales, Cuitlahuac, 1967–   ill. II. Title.
III. Series: Dobson, Danae. Forest friends series.
PZ7.D6614Fo 1993
[E]—dc20
                                                             93–10795
                                                                 CIP
                                                                  AC

Printed in the United States of America
3 4 5 6 7 8 9 LBM 9 8 7 6 5 4 3 2 1

HELP EACH OTHER

DANAE DOBSON
Illustrated by Cuitlahuac Morales

WORD PUBLISHING
Dallas • London • Vancouver • Melbourne

"Good night, Eric," Mother whispered as she kissed her little boy on the cheek. "Sweet dreams!"

Six-year-old Eric hugged his favorite stuffed dog, Tucker. It had been a long day and Eric was tired. Outside he could hear the rain on the rooftop. He closed his eyes to go to sleep.

Happy Birthday
Grandpa H
Grandma Bonnie
Andrew
Aaron Jeff
1996

Just then, there was a knock on the window. Eric sat up and looked around.

"What was that?" he said.

Tucker, the toy dog, began to growl.

"Shh!" said Eric. "Be quiet!"
Soon they heard the sound again. Slowly, Eric got out of bed and walked over to the window and lifted the shade.

"Why, it's only Sidney!" he said happily.

Sidney the Squirrel was one of Eric's friends that lived in Big Green Forest. The little boy smiled and opened the window.

"Hi, Sidney," he said. "What are you doing here?"
Sidney didn't look very happy.
"Eric, something terrible has happened in the forest,"
he said. "Your friends need your help right now!"

Quickly, Eric put on his clothes, his coat, and boots. Then he and Tucker climbed out the window and followed Sidney. "What's the matter?" asked Eric as they ran across the meadow.

"Well," said the squirrel, "Pinky fell into the river and can't get out."

"Oh, no!" said Eric.

Pinky was one of the rabbit twins. She was always getting into trouble. Eric knew she was in danger.

"Run faster!" he said as they made their way through the woods. Finally, they reached the riverbank. All of Eric's friends were waiting. There was Oliver the Skunk, Woodrow the Beaver, Fawna the Deer, and Pinky's twin brother, Pookie.

Pookie looked very upset.

"We've been waiting for you, Eric," he said. "My sister fell into the river, and we don't know how to get her out. Mother tried to save her, but she couldn't. We are so worried!"

In the distance they could see Pinky. She was sitting on a log in the middle of the river. And the log was drifting toward a big waterfall.

"Come on!" Eric said. "We've got to hurry!"

The animals followed behind him.

Mrs. Rabbit was running along the bank crying, "My baby! Somebody save my baby!"

Pinky looked very scared.

"Please help me!" she cried.

Eric saw a long tree branch lying on the ground. He picked it up and ran to the edge of the river.

"Pinky!" he called, "Jump in the water and grab this branch." The frightened rabbit shook her head.

"I'm afraid," she cried.

"You can do it!" said Eric. "Try hard!"

Pinky took a deep breath and jumped as far as she could. She grabbed the end of the branch with her paws.

"Good!" said Eric. "Now, everyone get behind me and pull hard."

The animals joined together and pulled as hard as they could. Even Tucker was helping.

At last, Pinky reached the riverbank and hopped out of
the water. The rain had stopped and the sun was peeking
through the clouds.

Mrs. Rabbit scooped Pinky in her arms and kissed her.

"I was so worried!" she said, wrapping her shawl around
the little bunny. "Thank you, Eric. Thank you, everyone!"

In the distance, they could see the log as it headed over the falls.

"That was scary," said Fawna. "It's a good thing Eric came to help us rescue Pinky. By the way, how did you fall in the river, Pinky?"

The little rabbit wiped a tear from her eye. "I was trying to pick some flowers for Mother," she said. "But I lost my balance and fell in the water."

Mrs. Rabbit smiled and gave her little bunny a hug.

"Next time look for flowers that aren't near the river," she said.

"Come on," said Sidney. "Let's go home now."

Eric and the animals began making their way back to Mrs. Rabbit's house.

"Look!" said Oliver, "a rainbow."

"It sure is," said Eric.

"What's a rainbow?" asked Pookie.

"A rainbow is a promise from God," said Eric. "A long time ago God sent a flood that destroyed the earth."

"Why did He do that?" asked Woodrow.

"Because people were evil and did many bad things," said Eric. "God was punishing them."

"Then what happened?" asked Fawna.

"After the flood was over, God put a rainbow in the sky. It was a promise—a promise that He would never cover the earth with water again."

"Does it still mean the same thing today?" asked Sidney.
"Yes," said Eric.
"How do you know so much?" asked Oliver.
"I learned it in Sunday school," said Eric.

The boy and his friends began walking toward Mrs.
Rabbit's house. Before long, they arrived at the front door.
"Say good-bye to everyone, Pinky," said Mrs. Rabbit.
"It's time for you and Pookie to have a warm bath and go
to bed."

"Thank you, Eric," said Pinky. "All the animals in Big Green Forest love you!"

"I think I hear my mother calling," said Eric. "I have to go home now."

"Good-bye, Eric!" said Pookie. "Come visit us again soon."

"Oh, I will," said Eric, "I will!"

The animals waved as Eric and Tucker headed toward home.

Just then, Eric opened his eyes. He was in his bed.
Tucker was still under his arm. It had all been a dream!

"Eric, come down for breakfast!" called Mother.

The little boy climbed out of bed and carried Tucker with him to the kitchen.

"Good morning," said Mother, giving him a kiss. "Look out the window. There's a beautiful rainbow in the sky."

Eric smiled as he remembered his dream . . . his very special dream with the friends of Big Green Forest.